Mr. McGratt and the Ornery Cat

Alex and Mackenzie, this one's for you. With love, M.H.

To Max with love. I hope you found a Mr. McGratt of your very own. — M.G.

Text copyright © 1999 by Marilyn Helmer
Illustrations copyright © 1999 by Martine Gourbault

Kids Can Press acknowledges the financial support of the Ontario Arts Council, the Canada Council for the Arts and the Department of Cultural Heritage.

Published in Canada by
Kids Can Press Ltd.
29 Birch Avenue
Toronto, ON M4V 1E2

Published in the U.S. by
Kids Can Press Ltd.
85 River Rock Drive, Suite 202
Buffalo, NY 14207

The artwork in this book was rendered in Prismacolor pencils.
Text is set in Sabon.

Edited by Laura Ellis and Debbie Rogosin
Designed by Marie Bartholomew
Printed and bound in Hong Kong by
Book Art Inc., Toronto

CM 99 0 9 8 7 6 5 4 3 2 1

Canadian Cataloguing in Publication Data

Helmer, Marilyn
Mr. McGratt and the ornery cat

ISBN 1-55074-564-6

I. Gourbault, Martine.   II. Title.   III. Title: Mister McGratt and the ornery cat.

PS8565.E4594M4   1999   jC813'.54   C99-930311-2   PZ7.H44   Mr   1999

Kids Can Press is a Nelvana company

Mr. McGratt and the Ornery Cat

Written by
Marilyn Helmer

Illustrated by
Martine Gourbault

Kids Can Press

Mr. McGratt had a cat. Actually it wasn't his cat. It came one day and decided to stay. But Mr. McGratt did not like cats. He especially did not like ornery cats, and this cat was ornery!

One morning Mr. McGratt looked out his kitchen window to see if the cat was still there. He didn't see the cat, but he did see a horde of pear-pecking starlings. They lined the branches of his pear tree, screeching and feasting.

Mr. McGratt rushed out to shoo them away. By the time he got the door open, the starlings were scattering like leaves in the wind.

That's when he saw the cat. "Scat! Scram! Skedaddle!" he shouted.

The cat didn't scat. It strolled across the yard and sat on the steps.

"Scat, cat!" said Mr. McGratt. The cat just yawned.

Mr. McGratt heard someone call his name. When he looked up, Ms. Mahoney was heading his way with her mail cart. "What a darling cat," she said. "What's her name?"

As Mr. McGratt started down the steps, the cat made a sudden dash toward the pear tree. Mr. McGratt almost tripped over it. "Ornery cat," he muttered.

"Mr. McGratt, that's no name for a cat," said Ms. Mahoney. "If she were mine, I'd call her Ann Marie. Ann Marie is the perfect name for such an adorable cat."

Mr. McGratt scooped up the cat and put it in Ms. Mahoney's cart. "You can name it anything you like," he said. "It's all yours."

"Thank you, Mr. McGratt!" gasped Ms. Mahoney. She kissed the cat smack on its nose. The cat's tail shot straight up in the air.

The next morning there was a knock on the door. When Mr. McGratt opened it, Ms. Mahoney was waiting for him with a jiggling box in her arms. She shoved the box at Mr. McGratt. "You can have your cat back," she said.

"It's not my cat!" said Mr. McGratt.

"I don't want him either," said Ms. Mahoney. "This cat is no Ann Marie. He's a tomcat. And he's anything but adorable." She hurried off.

"I never said he was adorable," Mr. McGratt called after her. "I said he was ornery." Ms. Mahoney didn't slow down at all.

The box flew open, and the cat jumped out. From the pear tree came the sound of flapping wings.

Mr. McGratt didn't even notice. "Scat! Scram! Skedaddle!" he shouted.

The cat didn't scat. He licked his paws and washed his face. Mr. McGratt went into the house and slammed the door.

For the rest of the day, Mr. McGratt was very busy. When he looked at the clock, it was well past four. "My newspaper," he groaned. "The Buswangers' dog will have torn it to shreds by now." He dashed outside.

Fluffy Buswanger was nowhere to be seen. But the newspaper was there and so was the cat, lying right on top of it.

"Scat! Scram! Skedaddle!" Mr. McGratt shouted.

The cat didn't scat. He stood up, stretched a long, slow stretch, and leapt onto the windowsill.

As Mr. McGratt reached for the newspaper, he saw Mr. Buswanger and Fluffy coming up the front path.

"Mr. McGratt, have you seen any stray dogs in the neighborhood?" Mr. Buswanger asked. "Fluffy's scared. He won't go out by himself today."

"No dogs," said Mr. McGratt. He glanced at the windowsill. "Just that cat."

"Nice cat," said Mr. Buswanger. "What's his name?"

The cat jumped onto the porch railing. As he landed, he knocked over a pot of geraniums. "Ornery cat!" spluttered Mr. McGratt.

"Mr. McGratt, that's no name for a cat," said Mr. Buswanger. "If he were mine, I'd call him Mon Ami. Mon Ami is the perfect name for such a friendly looking cat."

Mr. McGratt scooped up the cat and handed him to Mr. Buswanger. "He's all yours," he said.

"Thank you, Mr. McGratt!" Mr. Buswanger cuddled the cat. "Mon Ami and Fluffy are going to be the best of friends." The cat's ears flattened.

For the next three days, Mr. McGratt didn't see tail or whisker of the cat. He did see the starlings, but they flew off every time a shadow moved. Fluffy Buswanger came by, sniffed at the steps and scurried off without so much as one nibble at the newspaper.

On Saturday morning Mr. McGratt went out to weed his pumpkin patch. At lunchtime he made himself a sardine salad and sat on the porch to watch for the Gantry boy. Jason Gantry liked to take a shortcut right through Mr. McGratt's pumpkin patch.

Someone was coming up the street, but it wasn't Jason. It was Mr. Buswanger with the cat in his arms. "You can have your cat back," he said.

"He's not my cat!" said Mr. McGratt.

"I don't want him either," said Mr. Buswanger. "Fluffy's afraid of him. Mon Ami is not a friendly cat, Mr. McGratt." He plunked the cat at Mr. McGratt's feet and dashed off.

"I never said he was friendly," Mr. McGratt called after him. "I said he was ornery!" Mr. Buswanger didn't look back.

Mr. McGratt glared at the cat. "Scat! Scram! Skedaddle!" he shouted.

The cat didn't scat. He eyed Mr. McGratt's sardine salad. That's when Jason Gantry came running across the yard.

"Neat cat," he said. "What's his name?"

The cat snatched a sardine from Mr. McGratt's plate. "Ornery cat!" grumbled Mr. McGratt.

"Mr. McGratt, that's no name for a cat," said Jason. The cat purred as he munched the sardine. "He sounds like he's singing." Jason grinned. "If he were mine, I'd call him Harmony. Harmony is the perfect name for a cat like him."

Mr. McGratt scooped up the cat and put him in Jason's arms. "He's all yours if you'll stay out of my pumpkin patch," he said.

"It's a deal," said Jason. "We've got three cats at home, so Harmony will fit right in." The cat growled deep in his throat.

For the next week, Mr. McGratt watched for Jason to come running through his pumpkin patch. But Jason kept his promise. Mr. McGratt was a bit disappointed. He wanted to ask how the cat was getting along.

On Friday Mr. McGratt put the finishing touches on his wood carving and made himself a tuna sandwich. Before he had time to take a bite, he heard feet thumping across the porch. It was Jason with the cat.

"You can have your cat back," Jason said.

"He's not my cat!" said Mr. McGratt.

"We don't want him either," said Jason. The cat sprang from his arms. "He fights with our other cats. Mom says he doesn't know what harmony means."

"I never said anything about harmony," said Mr. McGratt. "I said he was ornery!"

"He'd make a great guard cat," Jason suggested. He sauntered down the steps and across the yard, neatly avoiding the pumpkin patch.

Mr. McGratt looked at the cat. Something told him that the days of pear-pecking starlings, newspaper-shredding dogs and pumpkin-smashing kids were over.

He broke his sandwich in half and put one piece on yesterday's newspaper. The cat came running.

"You are one ornery cat!" said Mr. McGratt.

The cat looked up at him. "Ornery ..." Mr. McGratt rolled the word around on his tongue. He liked the way it sounded. "*That* is the perfect name for a cat like you," he said.